# The Surprise Invitation

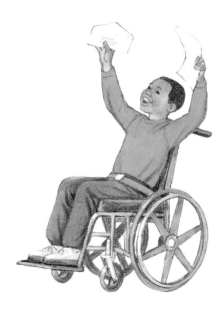

Story by
Dawn McMillan

Illustrations by
Al Fiorentino

Jon enjoyed watching basketball
on television.

But one day, he said,
"I wish I could play basketball
like that instead of just watching."

Jon's sister Nicola wanted to help him.
"Maybe there's something we can do,"
she thought.
Then she had an idea,
and she went to talk to Mom.

"Yes," said Mom, "I like that idea.
Let's write a letter,
but we'll have to keep it a secret."

Next week, something arrived in the mail.
It was addressed to Jon.
"It's an invitation!" he said,
"and it's from a basketball club!
They've invited us to a game
on Saturday night!  Why **us**?"

Mom and Nicola grinned at each other.

On Saturday, at six o'clock,
a car pulled up outside the house.

"It's time to go, Jon!" called Nicola.

When the driver of the car saw them coming,
he opened the window and called,
"Hi, Jon! I'm Ricky.
Your mom can help you into the car,
and your chair can go in the back."

In the car, Jon saw another wheelchair,
which was folded up
and buckled into the front seat.
"I wonder who that belongs to,"
he thought.

"Is everyone ready?" said Ricky.
"We can't be late,
because I'm playing tonight."

When they arrived at the stadium,
Ricky opened the driver's door.
He reached for his wheelchair
and lifted it out of the car.

"I'd better have my wheels!" he laughed.

Jon watched in surprise
as Ricky set up the wheelchair
and pushed himself into it.

"You're in a wheelchair,
but you can drive, too," whispered Jon.

"Oh, yes," laughed Ricky,
"this is a special car!"

Ricky took them through the crowds
inside the stadium
to some seats in the front.

"Now I must go and change," he said.

Jon looked around the stadium.
In the crowd
there were people with their faces
painted red and white.

Some people were waving flags
in team colors.

9

Suddenly Ricky's team
was coming out onto the court.

"Eagles, Eagles!" the crowd shouted.

Then, from other parts of the stadium,
the crowd screamed, "Sharks, Sharks!"
The second team was coming out
onto the court.

Jon's heart beat like a drum.
All the players were in wheelchairs!

The game started.
The Eagles raced up and down,
and they went spinning past the Sharks.

Jon yelled,
"Come on! Throw the ball!"

The Eagles scored goal after goal.
They were winning!

Then the Sharks took the ball.
They passed and bounced
and shot goals.
The score was even – 31 all!

"Come on, Ricky," screamed Jon,
"you can do it! There's still time!"

Ricky took the ball.
He sped down the court,
bouncing the ball as he went.
He threw the ball high into the goal
just before the final whistle sounded!
The Eagles had won!

Jon clapped and cheered,
and Mom and Nicola hugged each other.

Suddenly a voice came over the loudspeaker.
"Tonight we have a special visitor.
Please welcome... Jon Williams!"

The crowd clapped as Jon wheeled himself
onto the court.
Ricky passed the ball to him,
and Jon caught it.

"Have a go!" laughed Ricky,
so Jon bounced the ball back to Ricky.

The crowd cheered again.

"I think the Eagles might
have a new player one day,"
laughed the man on the loudspeaker.

Jon was so excited!
"Thanks for inviting me to the game!"
he called to Ricky,
and he sped back to Nicola and Mom.
"Now I know that one day
I will be able to play basketball
and drive a car!" he told them.
"I could even play for the Eagles!"